Always You

Elizabeth Grey

SNOWFLAKE
PUBLISHING

Please visit www.elizabeth-grey.com **to sign up to Elizabeth Grey's mailing list and for more information on her books.**

Facebook: www.facebook.com/elizabethgreyauthor
Twitter: www.twitter.com/elizabethjgrey
Instagram: www.instagram.com/elizabethgreyauthor

Always You - The Agency

Published 2017
ISBN: 978-1978186552

Set in 12 pt, Times New Roman.

Cover designed by Elizabeth Grey Art & Illustration of South Shields, Tyne and Wear, UK.

Copy Edited by Kia Thomas Editing of South Shields Tyne and Wear, UK.
www.kiathomasediting.com
www.twitter.com/kiathomasedits

For all the people who told me how much they loved
'Just Friends'

You made me a very happy bunny.

ACKNOWLEDGEMENTS

Thanks go to all my author friends who keep giving me brilliant ideas on how to get my name out there and get my books in front of the right people.

The journey is very long and sometimes lonely, but it makes it so much more fun doing it together.

Chapter One

SLOWLY I OPEN MY EYES. The haze of a late night coupled with a few beers pulls at my skull. What the fuck were you thinking Fraser? After working on the Thorne account until 11 p.m., I wanted . . . no, I deserved to sleep in my own bed tonight, but guilt led me here. Since I'll have to get up an hour earlier than normal to grab a change of clothes from my place before work tomorrow, I'm already regretting that decision.

My arm is numb. And it's trapped. Great. I squint at her clock – 4.30 a.m. Shit. I really need more sleep. My body craves it – my entire body, not just the dead arm. I adopt the moves of a ninja who drinks too much, pushing down hard into the mattress so I can free myself. Holy fuck, my arm hurts. How can the weight of someone so wee cause so much agony? I tense up as a searing-hot pain shoots the whole length of my numb limb and settles into the bones of my fingers. My hand transforms into a claw and I grip the duvet, hoping with every morsel of strength I have left in me that I don't wake her. Call me a wimp, but I don't want another frigging argument. The best-case scenario here would be one more hour of sleep, then getting the hell out of her flat *before* she wakes up.

I turn over. She stirs. My body goes stiff as her warm hand glides over my back and then circles my waist. How can she sleep like this? Her hold tightens around me and her knees nestle against the backs of mine. She must be some kind of sadist. Why me? Why did I ever think I could do this? I haven't had a girlfriend since I was at uni, yet here I am sleeping with a woman I've been dating for almost six months. No, scrub that – guilt-sleeping with her. I slept over last night because we argued on the phone and she cried. Yes, I know I'm an eejit.

There are some good things about having a girlfriend, of course. Sex on demand is one of them. Don't get me wrong, hitting on women in bars, clubs, work socials, is kinda top of my skillset, but it's hard work. Sometimes you just want to come home to something easy and familiar. I also take great pleasure in the fact my girlfriend is Zoe Callaghan – the sweet, perfect, extremely beautiful executive assistant to our CEO. Before we hooked up, Zoe was the talk of the creative floor, the one girl every guy wouldn't hesitate to take home to meet his mother. So, yeah, I'd be lying if I said I wasn't proud that I was the guy who got her.

Zoe stirs again and her breath puffs irritatingly on my back. I briefly consider waking her up and telling her to get over to her side of the bed, but demanding she shift when she's showering me with affection would lead to the emotional equivalent of a nuclear fallout. Zoe is the touchy-feely type. She directly associates sticking herself to my limbs with loving me. It's not – it's just fucking annoying. I'm sure most men would snuggle right back, but I'd rather drink a ketchup-and-shampoo smoothie. Christ, I'm an ungrateful bastard. Here I am in a proper adult relationship with the prettiest girl in the office, and I'm whingeing like a bairn who fell off his bike and scraped his knee. *Think positive thoughts, man. You're in bed with a beautiful woman, you stupid prick. The world's your octopus!*

I take a deep breath and snuggle back, attempting

this normal sleeping-with-my-girlfriend thing. After a minute I feel like I've got this, but then her hair tickles my back and I'm irritated again. How is her hair so scratchy? I may as well be sleeping next to a fucking Brillo pad. I clamp my eyes shut just as Zoe's flatmate's alarm goes off in the next room. Great, there goes my extra hour of sleep. And I need a piss . . . I guess that's me up then.

I do some kind of weird ninja-move out of the bed, but I tangle my leg in the duvet and yank the cover off Zoe. *Oh Christ, no. Please just let me get home with my head attached to my body. Don't wake up, Zoe, please.* She moans, and I do my best to push the duvet back over her, but I'm conscious that there's no time to waste. If I don't get to the bathroom before her flatmate, Tonya, then I'm doomed – she spends hours in the shower. I reach the door, realise I'm butt-naked, and . . . fuck, where are my boxers? I scan the floor, the bed, the chair . . . nothing. Fuck it. I grab a towel, sprint down the hallway and get to the bathroom just as Tonya shuts the door in my face.

Fuck's sake! Why is the world doing this to me? Rather, why is Tonya doing this to me? I know I pissed her off at a house party a few months ago. We – somehow – ended the night by playing a cheeky game of spin-the-bottle, and on my turn it landed on Tonya's sister, Jess. I kissed her – as per the fucking rules of the game, I might add – but Zoe got upset, so Tonya threw a drink over my head. I wouldn't care, but I didn't even find Jess attractive. She has a horse-face – like Tonya – but unlike her sister, she has a haircut last seen on a 1990s boyband member.

Zoe is still sleeping when I return from missing the bathroom. I get dressed quickly and quietly – without boxers – and I try to ignore the increasingly urgent pain in my bladder. God, I hate Tonya.

When I'm dressed, I watch Zoe for a moment – not "creepy" watch her, just kind of look at her and think about the direction my life is heading in. Is this where my younger self imagined I'd be at the grand old age of twenty-seven? My ten-year-old self would think I was gross for having anything to do with a woman, but then my ten-year-old self spent his days selling conkers to his classmates in a futile attempt to save up enough money for a pair of Air Jordans. That kid knew nothing. My twenty-year-old self would be far more impressed; after all, Zoe is undeniably hot.

As I think again about how lucky I should feel to be with her, a familiar sinking feeling twists my gut into a corkscrew. That feeling has always been there. It arrived the first time I kissed her and it never left. A constant nagging, twisting, stabbing mixture of guilt, regret and longing. Imagine what sleeping on a bed of nails feels like, then imagine you're strapped to the bed and you can't get off. That's what it's like – and it's my fault I lay down on that bed and my fault I got myself strapped to it.

And it's my fault I don't love her enough.

And it's my fault I allowed her to fall for me knowing she could never be *her*.

Zoe will never be Violet.

I let my eyes linger over Zoe's perfect body. Her creamy skin peeks from underneath the mint-green duvet, and my brain tortures me by imagining whiter skin instead – skin that looks almost too fragile to touch. I look at Zoe's soft brown hair, which frames her face in choppy waves, neat and glossy, the embodiment of Zoe's polished, refined personality. But all I can think about is darker, wilder, more unruly hair, tresses that personify everything there is to love about Violet – she's messy, complicated, enigmatic . . . different from everyone else.

Thinking about Violet in *that* way started as a guilty pleasure, but now it's a fucking torment. Violet is my best friend, my work partner and my teammate. She doesn't see me like *that* and she never will, and hell, I know I'm not good enough for her anyway. Nobody is good enough. So why can't I stop thinking about how amazing her skin looks when she wears only the tiniest touch of make-up? Why am I so crazy about those floaty boho dresses she wears all the time? Why do I think her legs look great in those amazing heels she defies gravity to walk in? Why do I love the way that little vein on the side of her forehead pops whenever she's thinking hard about something? And why does it feel like I'm cheating on her when I'm with Zoe, but it doesn't feel like I'm cheating on Zoe when I'm alone in my bed, dreaming about making love to Violet?

My thoughts are interrupted by the sharp close of the bathroom door. I wish Zoe sweet dreams, then I go for a piss. I find my pants hanging inexplicably on the heated shower rail. I'm probably too pleased by how warm they are when I put them on. It's a cold December morning after all.

***

"I can't believe you actually just said that." I hang my suit jacket on the back of my chair and sit down. Then I pick my jaw up off the floor. "There are some things in life that are just sacred. And that's one of them."

Violet peers over the divider between our desks. Her thick, black eyelashes flutter as she rolls her eyes. "You think movies are sacred?"

10

"That one is!"

I hear her suck in a breath to stop herself laughing. "I just don't see what all the fuss is about. You have to admit it's a bit melodramatic. And it's full of clichés."

"Melodramatic? It's iconic. A romance of epic proportions." I'm teasing her and she knows it. This is what we do – play each other, take the piss and try to gross each other out until one of us loses the game and we have a winner. I admit only to myself that the winner is usually her.

"Don't be ridiculous, Ethan. They only knew each other for a few days when the bloody ship sunk. What's epic about that?"

"The Titanic was epically big."

"And the iceberg was epically bigger. Oh wait, I get it – is this a penis-size, Freudian guy-thing?"

Now it's my turn to suck in a breath. If I laugh, I lose – the rules of the game we've been playing for over two years. I summon a light-hearted show of pretend outrage. "I also can't believe you saw the film for the first time last week. In case you need reminding, you're a girl, and girls are supposed to love this stuff."

"Well you seem to really love it, so what does that make you? Is there something you want to tell me?"

"Such as?"

"Are you absolutely sure you enjoy sleeping with women?"

I think back to last night. If she means literally "sleeping", then the answer is no, I bloody don't. I hate sleeping with women. If she means the other thing, then hell yeah, but I'd enjoy it far more if I were doing it with her. "Yes, I'm sure, but we're not talking about my likes and dislikes here; we're talking about yours. How the hell did you miss Titanic first time around? It was huge . . ." She catches my use of the word "huge" with a knowing wink. "Okay . . . it was epic."

She giggles and a jet-black curl falls onto her face. She tucks it behind her ear. "There was just something in the title that gave me an inkling the story wasn't going to end well."

"Wow. No shit, Sherlock."

"You know I only like happy films, Ethan. I avoided it."

"What changed?"

"*Heat* magazine. You know I hate celebrity magazines, right?" I nod as I think about the piles upon piles of glossy toilet-paper that Zoe flicks her way through every week. She calls it research, and it shows. Zoe dresses impeccably well on her secretary's salary. Her wardrobe is stocked with dresses also seen on the backs of celebrities she knows the zodiac sign and dating history of. Violet, on the other hand, thinks Anja Rubik is a kids' toy from the eighties and Juicy Couture is a smoothie blend. Yet she still manages to look amazing in every single non-designer outfit I've ever seen her in. "Well, there was a copy of it hanging around the dentists, so I had a look through and I started reading this article about Leonardo di Caprio and Kate Winslet. Did you know they've been best friends ever since they filmed Titanic? I can get *on board* – no pun intended – with a friendship like that."

"Aww, Vi, that's kinda sweet." I feel my face melt to mush. "Do they remind you of us?"

"What? Me and you?" she says with a delightful hint of tease in her tone that makes the corners of her mouth curl. "No, of course not. Kate and Leo are best friends. I see them more like me and Max."

"Very funny," I say as my phone pings. I lose my

train of thought, and the chance for a witty comeback about Max – our crazy artsy German colleague – evaporates. Damn. Guess I'll have to let her win this time. I tap on Zoe's message.

Took me all morning to find somewhere special for tonight – managed to book Carluccio's. Everywhere full for Christmas parties. Thank goodness Malcolm is out all day today and I only have that boring AGM meeting report to type up. Can't wait until eight! xx

Oh fuck, it looks like I'm going out tonight. Why am I going out on a Thursday? I should buzz through to her desk and plead the virtues of an early night, but given our argument yesterday, I'd rather have a bath in dog shit than cancel on her.

"What gives?"

"Hmm . . . ?"

"You look like a man who just drove over his cat and ruined his brand-new tyres."

She always has such a precise turn of phrase. "Zoe wants to go out tonight, but all I want is my bed. Does that mean I'm getting old?"

"Depends what you want to do in the bed."

"I want to sleep."

"Okay, then yes, you are getting old." She gets up from her seat, walks around the cubicle and perches on the end of my desk. My eyes are drawn to her cherry-red belt that cinches at her waist and coordinates perfectly with her lipstick. "You need to make up with Zoe, Ethan."

I don't try to deny it. This hitting-the-nail-on-the-head stuff women do really weirds me out. "How do you . . . ?"

"She told me twenty minutes ago in the kitchen. I apologised for letting work encroach on her time with you. She'll be fine, but still . . . you need to be . . . kind."

"You talk about me with her? I thought you didn't do female bonding?"

She scrunches up her nose. "I don't; she does."

I lean back in my chair and look up to meet her gaze. Her light-blue eyes sparkle under the bright office lights, and it hits me then that Violet is one of those women who has no idea how beautiful she is, which only makes her even more beautiful. "She just doesn't understand how things are up here, you know? She works on the exec floor – answering phones, typing letters and organising Malcolm Barrett's diary. It's a job for her, whereas . . . well, you know . . ."

"Advertising is your life."

"And it's yours too."

She lets out a little laugh and her boobs jiggle. I resolve to try to make her laugh again. "Nope, it's my job. It pays the bills."

"I thought . . ."

"Well you thought bloody wrong." She laughs again and – bingo! "Don't get me wrong, I love what we do here, but spending my life in this vipers nest with the CEO and our department head playing us off against each other is not exactly what I've always dreamed of."

"When they fight it's because they know we're the best creative team in the city and they both want to take credit for us. I'll even concede to you that Stella's far worse than Malcolm, even though Stella always has my back and Malcolm hates my guts."

I wait for her to speak with hope and – I'll admit – a smidgen of fear. Violet has never spoken about our careers like this before, and my stomach feels raw with nerves. I thought we were on the same page, but if

14

we're not, she might . . . Oh shit, I've never ever considered the possibility that she wouldn't always want to be a copywriter and work with me. She came here from New York, so she's already had a taste of the big wide advertising world. I came here straight from graduating UCL, slowly working my way up the ranks. I'm happy climbing the ladder, but what if she isn't? What if she goes back to the States? What if she leaves before I get the chance to tell her how I feel?

And fuck, why is that thought even in my head? I have a girlfriend, for fuck's sake!

"What is it?"

My throat contracts as I try to swallow. "Nothing . . . well, I just never considered you wouldn't always be walking on this path with me."

"Your path?" she asks. The faintest trace of a smile floats over her lips.

"Our path," I say as convincingly as I can. "I need you."

She sighs, then she locks me with sad eyes which look like they're trying to smile. "You don't need me for anything, Ethan. You think you do, but you don't. You have your dreams, and you've mapped out how you're going to make them a reality. It's unfair of you to expect me to want the same."

I open my mouth, ready to protest that I don't expect anything of her, I only hope, but she does something that removes my voice from my throat. She bends down and reaches for my hand, bringing it into her lap. My cock twitches, and . . . fuck, what was I saying about having a girlfriend again?

"Whatever happens in the future, we'll always be friends. You're the best friend I've ever had, and that means far more to me than a stupid job."

She gives my hand a gentle squeeze, the soft pads of her fingertips lingering a little longer against my palm than necessary – or is that just wishful thinking?

She returns to her desk, and I start mindlessly flicking between programmes on my computer, waiting for my brain to settle down and start functioning again.

Chapter Two

DIEGO VEGA, OUR CREATIVE DIRECTOR, catches me glancing nervously at my watch, and his dark eyes glint with mischief. "Well, well, I never thought I'd see the day when Ethan Fraser was under the thumb." He moves his arm as if he's cracking a whip and makes a "whit-chaa" sound. Irritating prick.

"You should know about being under the thumb, Diego. The last time we had impromptu drinks with a client, Mercedes called you ten times and said if you weren't home by midnight you were sleeping in the car. Didn't you kip at Daniel Noble's that night?"

He smiles at the memory, his thin, neat moustache curving up to his defined cheekbones. "Yes, and now you're in the same boat as me, Ethan." His Venezuelan accent makes his voice purr, accentuating the "th" sound in my name from deep within his throat. "This is how it all starts. I was twenty-one when I met Mercedes and twenty-four when my precious Ariel was born. But that was the day I realised the true meaning of life. It will happen to you too. I can see you and Zoe with a baby. You'd make a beautiful family, but let's hope the little one has her mother's good looks and personality."

I feel my cock shrivel up and die at the thought. Jesus, I can't think of anything worse. I have one hell of a lot of living to do before I make that bed and lie in it.

"Are you about to become a father, Ethan?" Nigel Bentley, Thorne Leisure's curly-haired, chubby-faced marketing director fixes an expectant gaze on me.

"No, Nigel, I am not going to be father. I am nowhere near 'going to be a father'. In fact, if

17

fatherhood were an island on Earth I'd be partying on the moon."

"Ooh, like that is it?" says Nigel with a smirk, and my brain throws up an image of my fist pounding his bulbous face into the table.

"It's not like anything. I have a girlfriend, that's all. It's not even that serious."

Violet frowns at me from the other side of the table as she knocks back her fifth glass of Chardonnay. Yes, I'm counting. Violet hates work socials, and alcohol is her coping mechanism. Only problem is she has the alcohol-tolerance level of a nun who hasn't eaten a thing since breakfast. Finding herself sitting next to our grim account manager, Sadie Fisher, and Thorne's insufferable commercial director, Dara Williams, is only going to intensify her survivor instinct and make her drink even more.

"It's not serious?" Diego laughs. "You stay over at Zoe's place every other night and she has a key to your apartment. I'd say that was very serious."

"No, it's just convenient."

"Alright, mate," he says in his weird half-Cockney, half-Caracas lilt. "You keep telling yourself that, but in the meantime, it's your turn to get the drinks in and I'll have the same again."

"Fine, but after this I'll have to go. I have a date at eight with my very casual girlfriend." I look over at Violet again. She pours herself another glass of wine as Sadie leans in close to whisper something undoubtedly boring into her ear. Violet's eyes glaze over and she mouths, "Save me".

I laugh to myself as I get up and go to the bar. I order another round of beers. I glance at my watch – again – and see that it's approaching seven thirty. When

18

Diego said we'd been invited out for after-work drinks to celebrate the end of the Thorne campaign and that my attendance was compulsory, I bloody well knew this would happen. We headed over to Pacifica at five, and I did the maths on the way: couple of hours of drinks and polite socialising, add on another half an hour as a safety net, then factor in traffic and distance between Covent Garden and Lambeth. Finally, given Zoe knows I'd be late for my own funeral, decide what would be acceptably late as opposed to unforgivably late. The upshot of all my maths is I'd have been in good time if I'd left fifteen minutes ago, so I hedge my bets and text her that I'm held up and need an extra half an hour.

The barman plonks the beers on the counter. I pay him and then pick all three bottles up in one hand so I can stuff my change into my back pocket with the other. Bad idea. A group of office workers wearing Santa hats barge through the doors behind me; one girl bumps me and a guy's ridiculous tinsel scarf ends up wrapped around my beer. "Hey, watch it," I yell at the guy in the cheap suit as he almost knocks the bottles out of my hand.

"Lighten up, mate, it's Christmas," he says. A duo of orange-faced girls with overly plucked eyebrows giggle as he pulls two baubles out of his pocket and starts juggling with them. What a fucking wanker.

"I'll lighten your fucking face with my fist, if you don't watch it," I spit back, my eyes narrowing in contempt.

I return to the table to find Violet missing and Nigel regaling the group with a story about Thorne's former CEO getting fired for soliciting an undercover police officer. I'd usually be up for hearing this kind of gossip, but I'm too preoccupied with scanning the bar for Violet. Has she sneaked away home while I was at the bar dodging out of the way of arseholes in cheap suits and Santa hats? I'll kill her if she has. I decide to finish my drink and leave too.

"So, Ethan," Dara says, her voice low and slurred with wine. "I thought you and Violet were an item when I first met you. You work so well together. I admit I'm a little sad that you have a girlfriend."

I feel my face turn bright red.

"Oh, everyone thinks that," Sadie says flippantly.

"Do they?" I ask, managing to inject some surprise into my tone, although I've caught the tail-end of office gossip about us many times.

"You know they do, Ethan," says Diego, "but luckily you have me as your manager, and I know Violet is way out of your league."

I smile, but I know it's the truth. "If you say so."

"I do say so, but what do I know? I think you're punching above your weight with Zoe too, but she seems to have fallen for you, so you must be doing something right. The other day Stella even commented on it."

Stella Judd is our head of department. She features between Diego and our CEO, Malcolm Barrett, on BMG's organisation chart. "Now, now Diego, no need to be jealous. You're happily married after all."

"I am, and that's why I know," Diego says with a wink.

"Know what? Diego, I have literally no idea what the hell you're talking about."

"I know you're with the wrong girl."

I slam my beer down on the table. "Diego, you're way out of line and, boss or not, if you say anything

20

like that again I'm going to be coming for your teeth. There has never – and will never – be anything between me and Violet. We're just friends."

Nigel, Sadie and Dara simultaneously inhale a sharp lungful of air. Diego takes a slow drink. My stomach knots. Diego is older than I am, but he's a keen boxer, so all things considered, threatening him with violence isn't a smart move.

"Okay, Ethan. I apologise for what I said. Now, I think it's maybe time you headed off to see your girlfriend, don't you?"

The inference is clear, and I know we'll probably be speaking about this tomorrow. For fuck's sake, why am I so belligerent? I take one last swig of beer, then leave the half-full bottle on the table, muttering an apology to Diego and a goodnight to everyone else.

I manoeuvre my way through the crowds of people – every single one of them three sheets to the wind on Christmas cheer and overpriced plonk. I hate everything about Christmas, except food and drink. The absolute worst of it is the trauma of shopping for gifts none of my relatives need or want. I've never yet had a fucking clue what to buy my mother. My tighter-than-a-gnat's-chuff stepfather gets whisky every year. He isn't Scottish like the rest of us, so I like to rub his nose in it. As for my half-sister, Esme is fourteen, which apparently means she's too old for Barbie but too young for wine, and I have no idea what comes between those two things. I have to enlist my brother's help every year. Rory is three years younger than me and far more in tune with his feminine side. He knows how to shop at Selfridges, so this year I threw money at him, deposited him on Oxford Street, then picked him up two hours later after he'd selected the perfect gifts for Mum, Esme and Zoe.

The only gift I never have any trouble buying is Violet's. This will be our third Christmas together, and I've actually enjoyed searching the internet for that perfect something for her every year. I've never found birthday presents difficult to buy either.

She's on my mind as I dodge my way past a trio of girls singing "Fairytale of New York". That song always sounds dreadful, but add a jug of mulled wine into the mix and it's the equivalent of Edward Scissorhands massaging a blackboard.

I twist out of the way of a couple singing into a wine bottle, and my eyes find her. She's standing at the bar talking to some guy. Fuck's sake, it would have to be Cheap-suit, wouldn't it? I stand and watch them for a moment. I want to say goodnight to her before I leave, but I can't bear to go over. She throws her head back and laughs at a joke he whispers into her ear and I want to be sick. He looks like he temps at a call centre, while she looks like some kind of ethereal mermaid, her jet-black hair falling in cascading curls almost to her waist. Surely she wouldn't go *there*? She wobbles on her heels as she laughs again, and he catches her elbow to steady her. Christ, how much has she drunk tonight? The barman passes her a clear-coloured cocktail instead of wine and my stomach does a back flip. *For Christ's sake, Violet, don't mix your bloody drinks. You have form for making hideous choices whenever you mix your drinks.*

There's no fucking way I'm leaving her with Cheap-suit, so even though my watch ticked past the number eight a while ago, I'm glued where I stand. Something about that guy bothers me. It might be his crinkly clothing, or it might be the fact he's shitfaced, or it could be the fact his eyes haven't left her chest the whole time he's been talking to her.

Violet hooks her handbag over her arm and picks up her drink. She says something to the guy, and his tongue pokes into the side of his cheek as if he's under the impression he's been given some kind of signal from her. I'm positive he hasn't, but is that just wishful thinking? My body instinctively moves forward a few paces, but then she totters away from him and I sigh in relief. She almost takes a tumble, and I step towards her, but Cheap-suit gets there first, grabbing her around her waist and pulling her into him. Her expression cracks with discomfort, and I practically throw some poor guy with a hipster beard and a man-bun onto his arse so I can get to her.

By the time I manage to cut through the crowd he has both of his arms clasped around her, his head is tucked into her neck and he's making her move to the beat of frigging "Mary's Boy Child". She tries to reach behind her to push him away, and I see red.

"Get your fucking hands off her now!" I roar. To his credit, he does as he's told.

"You again? What's your problem, mate?" he says, getting in my face. He raises his chin, and I think how easy, and totally fucking warranted, it would be if I sucker-punched him in the jaw.

"What's my problem? You're the one molesting my friend."

Violet positions herself between us. "Ethan, leave it. He got carried away and he's had too much to drink. I was handling it."

"You were handling it? His hands were all over you, and that's before we start on where the dirty perv's eyes have been all night." I turn to face the creep. He grins. I take another step towards him and he falls back, before retreating to his work colleagues.

"Ethan, I swear to god, I am so close to throwing this overly priced cocktail all over your overly stupid head! I told you I was handling it, so don't you dare make a scene. We're here with a client, for crying out loud."

My body tenses with frustration. I think I spend so long admiring Violet's insurmountably astonishing attributes that I forget she can be a stubborn, ungrateful pain in the arse too. "Don't thank me for getting that guy's filthy paws off you, whatever you do."

"He was just having fun, Ethan. I had it under control."

I look over at Cheap-suit. He's laughing and jeering at me as he drools over one of his tangoed co-workers, and it's a red flag to a guy who's having a mega-shitty evening. "Aye, you want to come here and tell me what you're laughing about, you creepy piece of shit?"

"Right, that's it, I'm going home. I'm bored, I'm drunk and you're being a wanker." Violet throws her drink down on the nearest table and strides towards the exit.

"Hey, wait up!" I leave my drink and immediately chase after her.

The dark sky glows gold under the streetlamps and a mass of Christmas lights. I walk behind her as tiny snowflakes float from the clouds and land like twinkling stars on her hair. I think it's the most beautiful sight I've ever seen and, for a moment, my breath gets caught in my chest. I pick up speed to catch up with her, and she stops suddenly, then she spins around and delivers a hard thump to my left arm.

"What the fuck was that for?"

"For making me leave that hellhole without my coat,

you dickhead! And why the hell is it fucking snowing?"

"Erm, because it's December."

She morphs into Miss Piggy and swings her handbag at me. Instinctively I grab her wrist. "Okay, okay, I'm sorry. Don't hit me again."

"Get off me," she says, struggling to break my hold, but I don't leave go. I take hold of her other hand, and she freezes. Our eyes lock, and my heart starts hammering in my chest as we stand in silence connecting . . . feeling . . . holding hands as if it's the most natural thing in the world for two workmates to be doing.

A single snowflake falls from the sky and lands on the end of her nose. She giggles, then her nose twitches, and if I wasn't completely sure that kissing her would be the craziest, most stupid thing I could ever do, I would be doing it.

And it scares me that I don't think I'd be thinking about Zoe if I did do it.

"Violet, I'm sorry," I say again, and it's true. I am sorry. Not for almost thumping that guy, of course. He deserved it. I'm saying sorry because she's cold, she's drunk and – most of all – I'm sorry that I can't tell her I'm totally, utterly, madly in love with her.

She takes out her phone. Her hands are so pale with the cold that they're almost translucent. I start to take off my jacket.

"Oh no," she says, wagging her finger at me. "Don't go all Walter Raleigh on me. Keep your jacket."

"But Vi, it must be zero degrees."

"Yeah, I know, it's December, remember?" she says as she taps on the keypad. "I'm texting Sadie to get my coat. I'm not going back in there where that . . . " She clasps her mouth tight shut, and I let out a short laugh.

"'Where that' what?"

"Nothing."

"No, not nothing. Finish that sentence, because I got you on this."

"I can't. I'm too busy texting."

"Violet . . ."

She sighs, taps her mobile a few more times, then tucks her phone into the pocket of her dress. "Fine. I'm not going back in there where that pervy guy is."

"Ha! I knew it!"

"That didn't give you the right to charge onto the battlefield like a bargain-basement Sir Lancelot deciding I needed to be saved. I'm no damsel in distress, Ethan."

"I know that, I'm sorry."

I'm tired of apologising now, and my stomach sinks because my arse is nowhere near Lambeth, so I know I'll have even more apologising to do by the end of the evening. Yet nothing is making me hail a taxi, because I'd rather be here with her, freezing my balls off in the middle of a London December with snow falling at my feet, than eating pasta in Carluccio's with Zoe.

Sadie ducks out of the bar with Violet's coat and goes back inside. Thoughts swirl around my head as I weigh up my options. I'd rather be with Violet than Zoe, but Violet doesn't see me in that way. Would she see me differently if she knew how I felt? I don't think it would matter, because deep down I know I can't be with her. I'm a shit boyfriend. I'd screw up her life, I'd destroy our friendship and she'd leave me. Truth is I'd rather have Violet, my best friend, by my side every day of my life than try to have a relationship with her, fuck it up and lose everything.

We walk around the corner and onto the main street.

She links her arm through mine for balance. A warm feeling hits me right in the middle of my chest because this just feels so right. We head for the taxi rank on Bow Street as the snow thickens and music from the Royal Opera House radiates onto the street. She stops still, closes her eyes, and her entire body seems to relax with joy as she listens. She smiles, and all I can think about is kissing her again.

"Do you hear that?" she says, practically breathing in the music. "*Norma*."

"Who the hell's Norma?" I know nothing about opera, whereas Violet can guess any aria in a single beat.

"It's the name of the opera. It's by Bellini. Just listen for a moment – she's singing 'Casta Diva', otherwise known as absolute perfection." She grips my arm tight as the haunting tune sweeps over us. "You must be feeling something. Tell me what you feel."

I definitely am feeling something, but given the physical sensation is located exclusively in my cock area as opposed to my musical-appreciation-brain area, I don't divulge. "It's nice, I guess."

"You're such a philistine." She playfully whacks my arm and rolls her eyes at me. "It's my dream to be a patron of the Royal Opera. I've been trying to save up the subscription for years. I almost had it, then my sodding boiler broke down and zapped all my funds. Bastard shitty luck." The vocals reach a high-pitched squeak that seems to go on far longer than is humanly possible. "Feel that?" she asks hopefully, closing her eyes again.

"Erm . . . well, I feel it in my ears."

She cocks one eye open and screws up her nose just as another snowflake lands on it. She swipes the cold droplet away as the music builds through its final crescendo. "You've spoiled my mood now. I was just about to say it was orgasmic."

Oh, sweet Jesus and holy fuckity fuck. Why the hell did she have to say that?

My phone pings. I retrieve it from my pocket as fast as I can, desperately trying to ignore the growing bulge developing in my pants.

"Oh fuck."

"What's up?" she asks as we join the end of the taxi queue.

"Zoe. She says she's gone home and . . . " I scroll further down the message. "She's going to find it hard to forgive me this time. Oh god, this relationship stuff is so fucking hard. I don't think I'm cut out for it, Vi."

"Well, I don't think she's being very fair on you."

I raise my eyebrows in surprise. Violet always backs Zoe – she calls it the "girl code". I call it bollocks, because if any of my guy friends were behaving like twats, I'd tell them straight, not apply a daft "guy code" rule. "You're taking my side in this? Are you feeling alright?"

"Aside from being pissed and just having had an orgasmic operatic experience, I'm entirely compos mentis." She snuggles her face into my jacket collar as a sharp wind twirls her hair around my shoulders. I inhale her scent – cinnamon and oranges, sexy as well as Christmassy. "Did you tell Zoe that Diego made us go out for drinks this evening?"

"Yeah," I say wearily. I'm resigned to the fact that I'm going to be spending yet another night guilt-sleeping at Zoe's – after she's chewed my head off and denied me sex. "I don't know why she was so insistent on going out tonight in the first place. Who wants to go out on a Thursday night with work tomorrow?"

Her forehead crumples into a frown. "Ethan, what's the date?"

"Fifteenth of December. Why?"

"Oh no, you idiot."

My heart misses a beat. "What do you mean? It's not her birthday."

"When was the Holland Carruthers summer party?"

All of a sudden the jigsaw pieces fit together. "Oh shit. It was June the fifteenth, wasn't it? We've been together six months today."

She slowly nods as the full horror sinks in.

A taxi pulls up, and I weigh up my options. Go home or go to Lambeth. "You take it, Vi. I'll get the next one."

"You sure? I think you might need it more."

"I'm sure. I have some thinking to do."

"Okay then." She gives me a friendly peck on the cheek and wishes me good luck. Then she climbs into the cab, and I watch her leave wishing I was going home with her.

Chapter Three

"YOU'VE GOT A FUCKING NERVE."

I'm greeted by Tonya's angry horse-face, and I wonder if I should have foreseen this encounter and brought a bag of oats to placate her.

"Can I come in?"

"No, you can't. I knew you were bad news from the start, Ethan Fraser, but I never thought you were this much of a bastard. Zoe's been crying all night, and I'm tired of you hurting her. You're not good for her."

"Look, I know I'm a shit boyfriend, Tonya. If it makes you feel any better, I'm a shit friend, colleague, son, brother and employee too. I've been apologising to people for being shit all night, and I'm not going until I get all my apologies done, so are you going to let me in or not?"

She folds her arms aggressively and purses her oversized lips. Christ, she's like the love child of Donald Trump and My Little Pony.

"It's okay, Tonya." Zoe appears from behind Tonya's shoulder, bearing puffy red eyes. My stomach knots.

"I'm sorry, Zo," I say, shortening her name affectionately. "I got held up. I was on my way to Carluccio's when I got your text."

Designated gatekeeper Tonya turns around and looks at Zoe, waiting for a signal. Zoe's teary eyes flit between us, and she nods her head. Tonya rolls her eyes and huffs. "Your funeral," she says as she flounces off.

What the hell does she mean by "your funeral"? I

was late for fucking dinner, that's all.

Zoe steps aside and we go into the sitting room. I flinch as Tonya's bedroom door slams shut. Damn, I hate Tonya.

I stand in the centre of the room, waiting for her to take the lead. She sniffs into a tissue. For god's sake, I know I'm a shit boyfriend, but isn't that a bit over-dramatic? She takes a seat on the sofa, next to a white artificial Christmas tree hung with red baubles. I notice for the first time that she and Tonya have gone to great effort decorating their flat. There're fairy lights strewn along the fireplace, a pair of wooden reindeers on the hearth, and a host of funny wee ornaments, including an entire nativity scene, on the window ledge. Her red tartan pyjama bottoms coordinate with her cute Santa top, so she's even managed to match herself to the room. I don't know how they can be bothered. The only thing I have is my beer "tree". My mum bugs me to get myself a Christmas tree every year, so this year I kept a few empty beer bottles, piled them on top of each other in a pyramid formation, and wrapped a piece of tinsel around them. Perfect festive cheer, via beer!

Zoe tucks one of her feet, clad in a fluffy pink polar-bear sock, underneath her. I sit down opposite her. "I had no choice about going out with the Thorne team tonight, Zo. Diego ordered my arse there."

"What time did you leave work?"

"Around five or six. Come on, you know how it is. Stuff like this is important, and if your boss tells you you're going, then you better bloody go."

"Was *she* there?"

I stifle a sigh. I sense she's trying to steer the argument in the direction she wants it to go in, and I'm not taking us there. Not this time. "If you mean Violet,

31

then yes—"

"Of course I mean Violet because it's always about Violet." The words tumble out of her mouth laced with venom. I've never seen her like this before. Zoe never loses her cool –ever. She's always calm, considerate and understanding. That's why she's so popular with everyone at work, men and women. She sniffs into the tissue again, her dark-blue eyes steely and determined. "She's always there, Ethan – right there in the middle of us. The third wheel. We had plans last night too, remember? It was even your idea to watch a movie and get takeout. You wanted to make up for having to go away – with Violet – at the weekend, but yet again you were *held up* at the office."

"Zoe, I had no choice about the weekend. There was a conference, and Diego—"

"I wasn't born yesterday, Ethan, so don't talk to me as if I'm stupid. I'm the CEO's secretary; I know the conference wasn't compulsory. You chose to go."

I feel my blood start to boil. What the hell is she trying to say? I open my mouth ready to protest, but then I check myself – she's right, I did choose to go. Sure, there was a work reason why I went, but I can't deny the biggest incentive was having a great weekend with Violet. "What do you want me to say, Zoe? Violet's my partner, we're good friends and we work well together. She'd hate it if she heard you talking like this. She really likes you."

"Oh, don't . . . don't you bloody dare try to make me feel guilty." She unfolds her leg and leans forward, resting her elbows on her knees. She bows her head. "I hate feeling like this."

"Like what?"

"Jealous." She practically spits the word out of her

mouth, it's so distasteful. "I hate feeling jealous, Ethan. I've never felt it before. It isn't me."

The guilt slams into me. I did this to her. I'm the most despicable human being on the planet. She lets out a sob, and I go and sit next to her on the sofa. She moves away from me. "Don't," she says in a whisper.

"Zoe, there is nothing between me and Violet. You're my girlfriend, it's you who I . . ." My voice crawls away and dies because I can't say it. I can't tell her I love her.

She turns to face me. Her beautiful heart-shaped face cracks and more tears fall. "You haven't told me you love me for weeks, Ethan. Did you think I hadn't noticed?"

"I guess things between us have been difficult, lately."

She nods but falls silent, her full lips parting slightly as she gets lost in thought. I wait patiently for her to speak, my stomach churning. I hate being the bad guy and I never wanted to hurt her. But, this is all my fault.

"Partner with someone else."

Her request cuts through me as if she'd sliced open my chest. "What?"

"Partner with Mohammed or Cass or Charlotte."

"Why on earth would I do that? They have partners already, so how the hell do you think that would work? 'Oh hey, Mohammed, I know you've just landed a huge client with Will, but Zoe's jealous of Violet, so will you work with me instead?'"

"Mohammed hates Will."

"That's not the fucking point!"

She shuffles away from me, as far into the corner of the sofa as she can go. "What is the point then? Because this, you working with someone else, is the only thing I can think of that will save us."

I stare at my feet and I feel it coming – the final goodbye. Isn't this what I've been wanting? "I'm not going to choose between you. What would I tell her?"

"You could tell her the truth."

My face burns as I consider that for a moment. I wish I'd drunk more tonight so I could get through this. "What truth? What are you trying to say?" I say wearily.

"You're in love with her, aren't you?"

"What? Of course not. We're just friends, Zoe – good friends." I'm so used to telling the lie that it drips off my tongue like honey.

"I guess we're over, then."

"Zoe . . ."

She raises her hand to silence me, and then she smiles. I'm thrown – I wasn't expecting that. "It's okay, Ethan. I knew tonight would end up like this. You haven't even mentioned our anniversary. Did you even realise?"

"I was reminded."

"By her?" She lets out a laugh, and I cringe because I just keep digging a bigger hole for myself.

"Like I said, Zoe, she'd be devastated if she knew you felt this way. She's never said one bad word about you."

"Maybe not, but I'm not interested in what she says. I'm interested in what she thinks."

"What do you mean?"

She rolls her eyes and shakes her head dismissively. My blood starts to boil. "She thinks she's better than me – actually she thinks she's better than everyone. And you know what, Ethan, I might be just a lowly secretary to her, but I understand people and everyone

34

likes me. She turns people off."

"Zoe, that's simply not true. That isn't who she is."

"I'm not surprised you're defending her," she scoffs.

"You're damn right I'm defending her, because *she's* the innocent party here."

She gets up, throwing a cushion to the floor as she stands. "Who *is* the guilty party then, Ethan? Me?"

I stand up to face her. My pulse is racing, but I'm not sure which emotion is driving the physical reaction – anger or guilt. "Blame me if that makes you happy."

"None of this makes me happy, Ethan." She walks towards the door, and I feel I need to say something to make her feel better, but I can't because I don't think there's anything I can say. She rests her back against the wall, one hand resting on the door knob, and I go to her. "Kiss me one last time before you go."

Okay, now this is hellishly awkward. Have we broken up, or haven't we? If we have, what kind of kiss does she want? A peck on the cheek? I've spent the last couple of days slowly reaching the realisation that I should not be in a relationship with Zoe, but now that it's happened – and she made the decision for me – I'm not sure how I feel. I know some part of me is relieved, but another part of me regrets not being able to make this work. And I'm not kidding myself here – I know I was abysmal. The relationship was a catastrophe, and I honestly don't think I'll ever be able to make it work, with anyone. I'm just not cut out for relationships.

I narrow the gap between us, but instead of kissing her, I take her hand. "Zoe, kissing you right now isn't a great idea."

"You don't want to?"

"It's not that." I sigh, my shoulders slumping. I search her eyes and remind myself that she's the one who's dumping me. "I think I should go . . ."

She kisses me then. Her lips covering mine as she glides her fingers through my hair and her tongue works its way into my mouth. I don't stop her. Letting her kiss me is the least I can do. Pulling away from her would hurt her even more, so I lean in and kiss her back.

Her arms are circling my waist now, the kiss growing in intensity. She untucks my shirt from my trousers and snakes her warm hands underneath. I lightly touch the base of her spine, wondering what the fuck I'm doing and whether I'll live to regret it. Her hands move down to my arse, then travel to my hips, holding me firmly against her. I start to pull away. "Zo . . ." It's all I can manage to say before her mouth is on mine again, hungrier and more adventurous than ever before.

"Just one more time," she says, her mouth rasping short, hot breaths against my neck as she nips softly at my skin with her teeth.

"We can't." I don't want to continue, which is unusual for me because I have form for shagging anything with a heartbeat. If I let her continue, I'm clearly going to get sex, but where would that lead us? When she unloosens my belt and reaches inside my pants, I know I'm in danger of letting her go too far. I have to stop this.

"Zoe, we can't," I say firmly, but with enough kindness in my tone to hopefully make her see I'm rejecting her in order to protect her.

She falls back against the wall as I zip up my trousers and fasten my belt, tears falling in rivers down her beautiful face. "I know." Her body shudders with sobs. "I just . . . I'm sorry . . ."

36

"It's okay, Zoe." I brush a glossy curl from her face and wipe the wetness off her cheeks with my thumbs. "Thank you for the last six months."

I don't look back when I leave.

***

The taxi ride from Lambeth to Kilburn takes over an hour and the best part of my wallet. I stop by the 24-hour mini-mart at the bottom of her street to buy a polite bottle of wine. This is definitely a stupid idea given the state Violet was in when we left Pacifica earlier, but I feel like I need to arrive with something.

Violet lives in a south-facing basement garden flat, which – she says – has the best aspect for growing wisteria in the entire city. I don't argue with her as I know fuck all about gardening, but I suspect the guy who tends the Queen's flower beds may have something to say on the matter.

Her neighbour's cat cocks its leg over a potted fir tree in her front yard as I descend the short metal staircase to her purple front door. I shoo the cat away, but then I smile as I realise I've got ammo – she hates Christmas, just like me, and she bet me twenty quid that she was more Scrooge-like than I was. When she saw my beer-bottle tree, she took my money without blinking an eye. Little did I know she had the fucking embodiment of all things festive sitting in a pot at the bottom of her steps.

I have to ring her doorbell three times before she answers, and when she does I suddenly worry about what I'm going to say to her.

"Ethan . . . what the . . . why are you here?"

She wraps a grey cardigan tight around herself, hiding the skimpy black camisole pyjama top I caught a peek at when she opened the door. She rests her head against the door frame and yawns so wide I can see her tonsils.

"Did I wake you?" I say with a laugh.

She yawns again. "No, but I was just about to head off to bed, so this better be good."

I walk inside her flat, and the warmth almost makes me pass out. I take off my jacket straight away. "Jesus Vi, it's like an oven in here."

"New boiler, remember? I haven't worked out how it works yet."

"How about when it gets too hot, you switch the bloody thing off?" I follow her into the sitting room and sit down on her plum-coloured sofa. I put the wine down on the coffee table and make myself comfortable.

"Actually . . . " she says as she sits down next to me and starts flicking through screens on her mobile, her face creased into a confused frown. "Now you're here you can help me with something. I may have . . . shit . . . okay, I *have* had a lot to drink tonight, and you know how my brain is a bit unfiltered at the best of times, right?"

She has that look on her face. "What have you done?"

"I may have sent someone a flirty text . . . Well, I think it's flirty."

I recline on the sofa. I love being at her place. It feels like home, even though her flat is nothing like my apartment. My studio is small, uncluttered and modern; every surface shines and every wall is brilliant white. I look around Violet's purple, gold and forest-green sitting room and I feel like I've been transported to the Shire – a grandfather clock with an irritatingly loud tick-tock, a cast-iron Victorian fireplace and a whole

38

wall full of books that Bilbo Baggins would have been proud of.

"What did the text say?"

She clenches her teeth and her eyes pop. "I don't want to tell you."

"Who did you send it to?"

"Erm . . . Eugene in Public Relations."

My stomach somersaults with nerves because Eugene – a red-haired Dubliner – is an artsy, poetic, opera-loving type, therefore totally up her street on paper. "Give."

She sheepishly passes me her phone then hides her face in her knees.

The last message was from him: *You're so hot I think even my jeans would fall for you.* Jesus Christ, that would give one of my best chat-up lines a run for its money! I scroll up to the top of the thread of messages.

Him: Just wanted to thank you for looking over that press release earlier. It was fabulous. How do you do it?

Her: Anytime x

Her again: I do it because I'm awesome.

Her yet again: And if you want me to look at anything else of yours, just let me know.

I drop the phone on my knee. "You filthy strumpet!"

"I know, I know, I know." She buries her head further into her knees and folds her arms over her ears. "Just tell me how to fix it."

I pick up the phone and read on.

Him: Is there anything specific of mine you want to look at?

Her: Not really, but I'd like to thank you for what you're showing me in my imagination.

"Oh no," I say, shaking my head admonishingly at

her. "Why did I let you mix your drinks?"

"He thinks I fancy him, doesn't he?"

"Ya think?"

She turns her head to one side and rubs her brow. "Shall I just leave it and hope it goes away?"

I put the phone down on the coffee table. "I think that might be your best bet. Maybe text him an apology tomorrow. Say you were shitfaced."

"Right, I'll do that first thing." She yawns into her sleeve. "Why are you here anyway? And why did you bring me more poison?" She points at the wine.

I laugh. "Force of habit. We don't have to drink it."

Her eyes scan mine, and I realise I'm single for the first time in six months, but I don't want to tell her how it happened. If I told her any of what Zoe said about her tonight she'd be devastated, and she doesn't deserve to feel like that. This isn't on her – it's on me.

"I broke up with Zoe."

"Oh no, that's awful. I'm so sorry, Ethan. How did she take it?"

She swings her body around to face me, and her thigh presses against mine. The subtle, non-sexual contact makes the blood rush to my cock like I'm a horny teenager.

"Not very well. She's upset." She places her hand on my knee, and the skin at the tip of my cock tightens. Christ, what's wrong with me? "I was a shit boyfriend, Vi. It's all my fault."

"Hey, no you're not. You just haven't met the right girl yet. I like Zoe, but . . . well . . . she was maybe too perfect."

"You've never said that before."

"It wasn't my place to say anything – if you loved her." She smiles kindness at me, and all I want to do is kiss her. Oh, and rip her clothes off.

"I don't think I ever loved her."

She gives my knee a sympathetic squeeze. "You'll find the right girl one day."

A lump forms in my throat because I know I've already found her. It was always her, always Violet. "I wish I'd told her sooner. I'm terrible at this, aren't I?" I say with a self-deprecating laugh. "I'm totally fucking hopeless."

"You're talking to someone who just smut-texted Eugene in Public Relations and I don't even fancy him – he has a scratchy orange beard and his nose is too long. If you're hopeless, then you're in good company."

Our eyes meet, and it's like it was earlier in the street outside the Royal Opera – a connection. Something tangible hanging between us that tells us both that we get each other better than anyone else ever will.

"Wanna stay here tonight?"

I nod. "My wallet is empty. I spent all my money on the taxi over here and that bottle of wine."

She heads into her bedroom and reappears with two pillows and a blanket.

I notice it's still snowing outside. I get a very strange feeling that can only be described as "festive", but then my stomach sinks. "Oh, shit . . . it's Christmas next week. I was going to spend the day with Zoe. My family is cruising the Med this year. Well, except for Rory, who's working at the bar. He gets quadruple time apparently."

She plumps the pillows as she places them on the sofa for me. "If you're stuck you could always come here."

"That'd be amazing, if you're sure?" My heart starts

leaping up and down in my chest like I've a little Christmas elf living in there. Do elves leap? No, wait, that's pixies. Is it? Oh, fuck knows. "I wouldn't want to gatecrash any plans you might have had."

"I didn't have any. I always spend Christmas alone. It's a Violet thing."

"Well, as long as I'm not gatecrashing your Violet thing, I accept." I start taking off my shirt. Her eyes linger on my chest for a split second, then she quickly looks away.

"Good," she says, beaming a huge smile. "I'll leave you to it. Leave your undercrackers on under the blanket. I don't want to go for a pee in the middle of the night and get a nasty surprise."

She retreats to her bedroom. I watch her, transfixed by the way her hair bounces as she walks. "You owe me my twenty quid back for that giant fuck-off Christmas tree sitting outside your front door by the way."

"No I don't," she says, closing her bedroom door. "It isn't a Christmas tree, is it?"

"It's a fir tree," I shout. "That's the dictionary definition of a Christmas tree."

"Do you see any lights, tinsel, baubles or a fucking angel on it, huh? No, you don't, so shut up and get some sleep."

I lie awake for hours thinking about her.

I imagine walking into her bedroom, declaring my love for her and gathering her up in my arms. I imagine her waking me up to tell me she's been secretly in love with me from the first day we met. I let my mind torment me with dozens of scenarios that might force me to tell her how I feel about her, but fear brings me back to reality. I *would* fuck up. I *would* lose her.

But it was always you, I repeat in my mind.

I close my eyes. Her scent lingers on the pillows beneath my head. I breathe her in as I fall asleep.

THE END

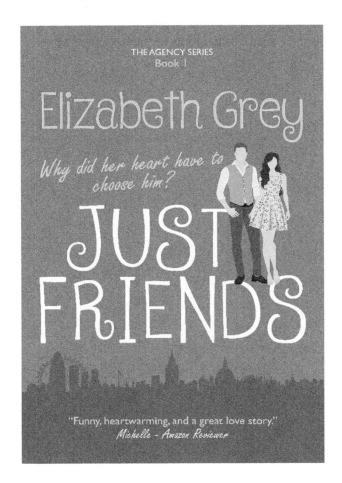

Just Friends
The Agency – Book One

Violet Archer has her dream job at one of London's top advertising agencies, and the fact she gets to work with Ethan Fraser every day makes it even better. He's the best friend a girl could have. And she's never even noticed how hot he is. Nope. Definitely not.

When a big night out deteriorates into a great big mess, Violet's world starts to wobble like a drunk giraffe on stilts. She's caught in a web of secrets, none of which are hers. And maybe she is starting to notice how hot Ethan is after all. And sweet and kind and... oh dear.

Has Violet fallen for her best friend? Can their friendship survive yet another secret? And, the question Violet is most scared to ask, could Ethan have feelings for her too?

This raunchy, hilarious rom-com is the first in The Agency series by Elizabeth Grey.

Read on for a preview.

Just Friends – Chapter One

IT'S ONLY TAKEN THREE MONTHS, two weeks and five days, but here I am – in Stuart Inman's Notting Hill bedroom, wearing underwear that screams 'sex goddess' and a spray tan that shrieks 'never again!'

Thankfully Stuart is too busy burying his head in my cleavage to notice my tangerine armpits and stripy inner thighs. He's also groaning and purring and nuzzling and . . . okay, I'm not really sure what he's doing down there, but I hope he tries another move soon. I can think of much better things I'd like him to do to my boobs than use them as a pair of earmuffs.

Ah, good, he's heading north now. I look into his deep blue eyes and remind myself why I'm here. Stuart Inman is hot. Think Matt Damon in an action movie: all blonde and ripped and gun-toting. Matt Damon, that is, with the gun-toting. Not Stuart. The only thing Stuart totes is a rather feminine Burberry man-bag.

He backs me up against his bedroom wall and I run my fingers over the taut muscles of his fabulous chest. Then I feel his lips brush against mine, his tongue darting in and . . . oh, sweet Jesus, what the . . . ?

Breathe. Close your eyes, think of England and for heaven's sake, just breathe . . .

What in the name of all things holy was that? If it was supposed to be a kiss, then please don't let him kiss me again. Talk about disappointing. Has he been practising his make-out skills with a bathroom sponge? I've kissed a few men in my life, and most of them have been far less confident, successful and drop-dead gorgeous than Stuart Inman, so how is it possible that he kisses like a half-starved pufferfish devouring a shrimp? Ugh . . . no. Just no.

I run my fingers over his abs, trying to avoid his hungry mouth. So what if he's a crap kisser? We can work on the finer details later. The important thing right now is sex is happening – my eight-month-long drought is coming to an end and my velvet-touch, thirty-function, silicone Raunchy Rabbit can hop off into the sunset and do one.

His hands move over my body as he lowers me onto his bed. I look into his eyes, his cheeks dimpling as he smiles seductively. I should be kissing him, feeling him, touching him until we're both sweaty and panting for more, but my stupid brain decides to torture me instead: *Stuart kisses like a pufferfish. Stuart kisses like a pufferfish. Stuart kisses like a pufferfish* . . . and . . . oh no, he's nuzzling my boobs again . . . and oh my god! What the hell was that? Why are his pants stuck to my stomach? Oh shit, he has, hasn't he? He's shot his load. He rolls onto his back with a thump. "I'm sorry . . ." he whimpers.

I don't know whether to laugh or cry. Where's my Matt Damon action hero gone? Why does the fittest client I've ever worked with have less knob control than a horny teenager who's just discovered Pornhub? What did I do to piss off the gods of shagging this time? Could life be any more bloody unfair? Come back, my beloved Raunchy Rabbit, I miss you already.

He turns to face me, but I don't want to look at him. Yes, I'll admit, I'm a coward. I can't think of anything good to say, which, given words are my livelihood, is pretty pathetic.

"You're just so hot. I'm sorry. I couldn't help it." He removes his sticky pants to reveal an appendage that could accurately be compared to a half-eaten Walnut Whip – sad, shrivelled and hollow. He crosses his legs in an attempt to hide his shame, and sadly, it doesn't take much to hide *it*. How on earth didn't I notice that before? I usually check out a guy's bulge before I commit, don't I? Jeez, this must be the most desperate for sex I've ever been in my entire life.

"It's okay. Maybe next time?" I say, with the kind of insincere politeness a politician would be proud of.

"I can still go on. Just give me a minute," he says with an enthusiastic tug to his manhood, and my stomach lurches. Do I want to have sex with a Matt Damon lookalike if he's only packing a chipolata and kisses like a pufferfish sucking on a sponge?

Ten seconds later, he's sliding his hand into my knickers and frantically rubbing away at what I'm sure he thinks is my clitoris, but of course, it isn't. The gods of shagging wouldn't be that merciful. I simulate a few polite moans and consider following through with a fake orgasm, but as he's jabbing the inside of my leg with the elbow of the hand that's futilely attempting to transform the chipolata into a frankfurter, I can't take it anymore.

Mission abort! Mission abort!

"Okay, stop. Just stop," I say as I squirm out of his grasp.

He removes his hand from inside my underwear and frowns at me. "What's up?"

"Um . . . that's not really doing much for me. Sorry."

"What do you mean? What's wrong with you? I always get girls off doing that."

I feel my eyes pop. "Really?"

"Yeah, really," he replies with an eye roll and way too much attitude. All of a sudden I have too many words, but as none of them are kind, I swallow them down and start putting my clothes back on.

Stuart tuts, gets up and pulls on a robe. I leave his apartment as fast as I can and head towards Holland Park Tube, flagging the first taxi I see on the way.

***

At times like these, a girl needs her best friend, so I direct the taxi driver to the heart of the West End and make my way to Ethan's Soho penthouse. I check my watch – it's 1:15 a.m., but it's Friday and he said he was hosting a get-together with the lads tonight, so he might still be up. If he is, I hope he's alone.

I say hi to Gus, the doorman of Ethan's building, before taking the lift to the top floor. I listen at the door – silence, thank goodness – and ring the buzzer. And then I ring again. And again . . . until finally the door opens to reveal a bare-chested Ethan clad only in tartan pyjama bottoms, his usually perfectly styled dark hair sticking up in a hundred different directions and the aroma of beer lingering on his skin.

"Vi?" He rubs at his eyes. "What time is it?"

"Um . . . late—"

"Are you okay?" he interrupts, panic rising in his voice.

"Yes, of course. I just . . . I'm sorry. I didn't think you'd be in bed yet. I'll go. We can talk tomorrow." I turn on my heel, feeling stupid for coming over in the middle of the night.

"Wait," he says, his voice still gravelly with sleep and his Scottish accent more pronounced than usual.

I turn around. He's looking at me as if I've grown an extra head. "Why are you looking at me like that?"

"Just wondering what you've done this time."

I scowl at him, and he beckons me into his apartment with a knowing grin. I head straight for the open-plan sitting/eating/sleeping room to find his very stylish bachelor pad has morphed into a students' union den – empty beer bottles, pizza boxes, lad mags, overflowing ashtrays, women's underwear . . . Whoa! What?

"Do you have a woman in here?"

"No, of course not," he says, pulling a t-shirt on over his head.

He looks confused. I don't want to ask, but the question is begging. "Have you had a stripper in here?"

"Eh? What are you talking about?" He looks absently around the room until his gaze finally settles on the skimpy fuchsia-pink pair of knickers sitting proudly on the coffee table. "Ah. Those are here courtesy of Max."

I dread to think. Max is my other best friend, and he was Ethan's roommate in halls at UCL. We've all worked together at Barrett McAllan Gray, one of London's largest ad agencies, for the last three years. Max is a designer; Ethan and I are a creative team – he's the art director and I'm the copywriter.

"Did Max have a woman in here?"

Ethan laughs. "Yeah, sure. Max had sex with a woman in my apartment and we all sat around and watched. Actually, now I think about it, that sounds like a fun night."

I stifle a giggle. "You want to watch Max having sex?"

"Ew, what? No. I didn't say that. In my mind there would be two women . . . and we'd all be naked . . . you know. And I'd get to do stuff too."

I stare at him open-mouthed, wondering why my life is plagued with teenage men.

He exhales in defeat. "Okay, I did say that, didn't I?"

I tumble onto his grey sofa in a fit of giggles, hugging his favourite Beatles *Yellow Submarine* cushion. "Yep, you did. But I know what you meant."

He slumps down next to me. "The knickers are Ruby's."

"Oh my god, no. Ruby and Max? My Ruby? My trainee and therefore my responsibility? Please tell me he hasn't." Ethan shakes his head, but I'm still questioning Ruby's sanity.

"No, it's not like that. It was Will."

"Will? That's not much better. He's horrible with women."

"No, you don't understand. It was a dare. She doesn't know we have them."

I stop laughing. We've been here before and it doesn't end well. The last time Max and Will pranked each other it ended up with a written warning from the CEO. "Ethan Archibald Fraser, confess your sins now. Have you and your merry band of fuckwits done anything gross, cruel or in any way misogynistic to poor Ruby?"

He nods his head and burps. A cloud of rotten-beer belch fills the air. "I would have to plead guilty on all three counts."

"Oh my god, you're such a dick."

"I know, and don't call me that."

"What? A dick? I could call you a lot worse."

"No, don't call me Archibald. I know I'm a dick."

I prop the giant cushion behind my back and make myself comfortable. "Just get on with the story."

Ethan contorts his face into an aggravated scowl and moves closer to me. I smile inwardly because I can tell he's trying not to laugh. He also has an unmistakeable glint of mischief in his eye, reminding me why we've been inseparable since the day we met: we get each other, trust each other, laugh at the same things, and as a result, we're the best advertising creative team in the city.

"Max has a thing for Ruby, apparently. He heard she needed help decorating her bedroom, so he volunteered. Will found out and teased the shit out of him. Mohammed joined in, it escalated, and the guys ended up betting Max he couldn't steal an item of clothing from her bedroom drawers." He points at the pair of knickers and chuckles. "Max won, so Mohammed owes him fifty quid."

"Let me get this straight – Max stole Ruby's knickers to win a bet? That is so disrespectful. I'm disappointed in Mohammed. You, Max and Will are a trio of shits, but Mohammed has always been a gentleman. Was he here tonight?"

"No, he's left."

"Left what?" I ask in confusion.

"Barrett McAllan Gray. Didn't anybody text you tonight? He pissed off a client – nothing major – but Will had a real go at him after you left work this afternoon, and he walked. Said he wasn't working with a sociopathic megalomaniac any more. It turns out Mohammed's flatmate works for the Daily Mail and he's landed a great copywriting job there already."

"Oh my god!"

"I know. I'm going to miss Mohammed. He was a good laugh."

"No, I mean, oh my god, the Daily Mail hired someone called Mohammed? What's up with that?"

He laughs and runs his fingers through his short, feathery hair. "So, I take it things didn't go too well with Stuart."

"It was a disaster," I reply, not meeting his gaze. "No, it was worse than a disaster."

Ethan raises an eyebrow and his smile fades. "Worse than your date with Eugene from Public Relations?"

Oh flip, I'd forgotten about him. After an unbelievably great evening – at The Ivy, no less – Eugene somehow slipped in the gents' toilets, cracked his head open on a urinal and had to be stretchered out. "Yes, it was worse than that. Much worse."

"Oh shit," he says. "Well, I always thought Stuart was a tube."

"A what?" I twist my face in confusion. "You thought he was an underground train?"

"No, a tube's an idiot – Scottish slang."

"You haven't been anywhere near Scotland for sixteen years. Speak the Queen's English, for goodness sake."

"Hey, I'll always be a proud Scotsman. Now, are you going to tell me what Stuart did, or are you just going to insult my vocabulary?"

I inhale deeply for courage. "You have to promise not to tell anybody."

"Of course," he says, and being a good Catholic boy who never goes to church and doesn't believe in God, he crosses himself for good measure.

"I don't know where to start, so I'm just going to blurt it out, okay?"

"Um . . . okay."

"Okay." I take another deep breath. "So, despite being blessed with the body and looks of a demi-god, Stuart Inman is a crap kisser, he's hung like a gerbil in a blizzard and he shot his load before I even got my knickers off."

Ethan covers his mouth with both hands and starts to turn purple.

"Don't you dare bloody laugh!"

He laughs. Actually, he doesn't just laugh. He wheezes, shrieks, coughs, splutters, almost chokes and then runs to the bathroom saying he needs a piss. It takes a solid five minutes for him to compose himself and I can hear him laughing the whole time he's in there. When he finally emerges he apologises, whilst trying not to laugh, and then he sits down and proceeds to start laughing again.

"It isn't funny. I'm totally mortified, and we still have to work with Stuart. I pretty much told him he was a shit shag and ran away. Does that make me awful?"

"Um . . . yeah, a little bit," he says between giggles. "I'm sorry, but who'd have thought it? Now I know why he drives that ridiculous Porsche."

"I won't be able to look at him ever again without replaying it. And seeing, you know, *it* . . . oh, crap. Life is teaching me a lesson here. Can you remember when I passed that law last year after Eugene? 'Never screw around with people you have to work with.' Why didn't I stick to it? We have to see Stuart tomorrow night at that blasted awards show. Or rather you do. I'm not going. I can't face it."

"Oh no you don't. No way are you getting out of the AdAg Awards. You've been trying to find an excuse not to go for months. In fact, I wouldn't be surprised if you orchestrated this whole Stuart thing deliberately."

"You think I shrank Stuart Inman's penis to get out of going to the AdAg Awards?"

"Stranger things have happened."

"Have they? Where was that then? In darkest voodoo-magic land?"

He shrugs, but his expression changes back to pity again. "Do you want to sleep here tonight?"

The mention of sleep suddenly makes me feel exhausted. I shuffle down on the sofa, curl up into a ball and nuzzle my cheek into Ethan's super-comfy Beatles cushion. "Thank you, that would be nice."

"You can have my bed if you want."

"That's okay. I'll be fine here."

"Okay, I'll get you a blanket."

He disappears over to his bedroom, which is around the corner of his L-shaped open-plan studio. He returns with a dark-orange knitted throw and drapes it over me. Then he perches at my feet and rests his hand on my curled-up knee. "I *am* sorry about tonight," he says softly.

"Even if Stuart's a tube?"

"Yeah, sure. I mean, you can do much better than him, but I want you to be happy."

"Thanks, Ethan. I just hope I haven't screwed things up for you at work."

"Well, if you need advice from an expert, just pretend it didn't happen and go on as normal. That's what I do. And I have a lot of experience sleeping with clients, and co-workers, and—"

"And the models we hire. And actresses. And the woman who scrubs the office toilets."

"That only happened once, and Kiki is a very lovely girl."

"She doesn't speak a word of English."

"She speaks the language of love."

I groan and turn over as he laughs and pats my knee.

"Look at it this way, Vi. The fact Stuart shot his load before the main event means you must be pretty damn hot in bed."

I play along. "Maybe I am, but you'll never find out."

"Why not?" he teases.

"Because I have to start obeying my law, so I'm not just swearing off dating men I work with; I'm swearing off all men, everywhere. I'm going to enjoy being single until I'm at least thirty."

"Well, that's a shame," he says with a chuckle, tucking the blanket around me. "And just for the record, you are hot. You're the hottest woman I've ever met."

What the hell? My stomach flips, and I have no idea why it's flipping because Ethan and I joke like this all the time. I close my eyes and listen to the sound of his feet padding over to his bed, followed by the creak of his mattress as he climbs in and gets comfortable. And just for a very brief fraction of a moment I imagine joining him.

My eyes fly open in surprise. I must be really bloody hard up if my brain is thinking about my best friend in this way. Thanks a lot for breaking my brain, Stuart Inman!

I push it out of my mind and fall asleep to the strangely comforting sound of traffic mixed with spring rain falling on the windows.

Do Ethan and Violet make it?

Buy Just Friends online from retailers to find out.

It's Complicated - The Agency #2

Could you keep your love secret?

THE AGENCY SERIES
Book 2

Elizabeth Grey

IT'S
COMPLICATED

Sometimes love
isn't enough

"From the first page until the last, I was hooked!"
Alison – Amazon Reviewer

Did you enjoy this FREE ebook?

Please leave me a review at Amazon.co.uk and/or Amazon.com to let other readers know all about **'Always You'**.

Printed in Great Britain
by Amazon